# The Lot at the End of My Block

**Kevin Lewis**   •   illustrated by **Reg Cartwright**

HYPERION BOOKS FOR CHILDREN

New York

First Edition
1 3 5 7 9 10 8 6 4 2
Printed in Mexico

The text for this book is set in 17-point Akzidenz Grotesk.

Library of Congress Cataloging-in-Publication Data on file.

ISBN 0-7868-0596-X (trade ed.). — ISBN 0-7868-2512-X (lib. bdg.)

Visit www.hyperionchildrensbooks.com

For Bonnie's Robbie, Lauren's Owen,
Michelle's Daniel, and my Phil — K.L.

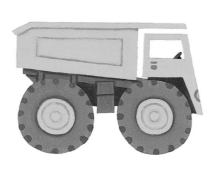

For Caroline Shaw — R.C.

This is the lot at the
end of my block.

These are the workmen

who came to the lot

at the end of my block.

This is the wall
built by the workmen
who came to the lot
at the end of my block.

Here is the hole

made in the wall

that was built by the workmen

who came to the lot

at the end of my block.

This is the pit, all dusty and deep,

that I saw through the hole

that was made in the wall

that was built by the workmen

who came to the lot

at the end of my block.

This is the dump truck,

moving dirt from a heap,

on the side of the pit, all dusty and deep,

that I saw through the hole

that was made in the wall

that was built by the workmen

who came to the lot

at the end of my block.

This is the shovel that backs with a beep

and fills the dump truck with dirt from the heap

on the side of the pit, all dusty and deep,

that I saw through the hole

that was made in the wall

that was built by the workmen

who came to the lot

at the end of my block.

This is the bulldozer that crawls at a creep

and makes piles for the shovel that backs with a beep

and fills the dump truck with dirt from the heap

on the side of the pit, all dusty and deep,

that I saw through the hole

that was made in the wall

that was built by the workmen

who came to the lot

at the end of my block.

This is the crane, swinging so many feet

above the bulldozer that crawls at a creep

making piles for the shovel that backs with a beep

and fills the dump truck with dirt from the heap

on the side of the pit, all dusty and deep,

that I saw through the hole

that was made in the wall

that was built by the workmen

who came to the lot

at the end of my block.

This is the girder that is moved by a sweep

of the arm of the crane, swinging so many feet

above the bulldozer that crawls at a creep

making piles for the shovel that backs with a beep

and fills the dump truck with dirt from the heap

on the side of the pit, all dusty and deep,

that I saw through the hole

that was made in the wall

that was built by the workmen

who came to the lot

at the end of my block.

This is the welder using heat

to attach the girder moved by a sweep

of the arm of the crane, swinging so many feet

above the bulldozer that crawls at a creep

making piles for the shovel that backs with a beep

and fills the dump truck with dirt from the heap

on the side of the pit, all dusty and deep,

that I saw through the hole

that was made in the wall

that was built by the workmen

who came to the lot

at the end of my block.

This is the mixer that mixes concrete

to pour when the welders are done using heat

to attach the girders moved by a sweep

of the arm of the crane, swinging so many feet

above the bulldozer that crawls at a creep

making piles for the shovel that backs with a beep

and fills the dump truck with dirt from the heap

on the side of the pit, all dusty and deep,

that I saw through the hole

that was made in the wall

that was built by the workmen

who came to the lot

at the end of my block.

This is the building.

It's finally complete.

The mixer's done mixing and pouring concrete.

The welders have finished. They're done using heat

to attach the girders that were moved by a sweep

of the arm of the crane that swung so many feet

above the bulldozer that crawled at a creep

and made piles for the shovel that backed with a beep

and filled the dump truck with dirt from the heap

from the side of the pit, all dusty and deep,

that I saw through the hole

that was made in the wall

that was built by the workmen

who came to the lot

at the end of my block.

And here's my new buddy—
we happened to meet
when he moved to the building
just built down my street.

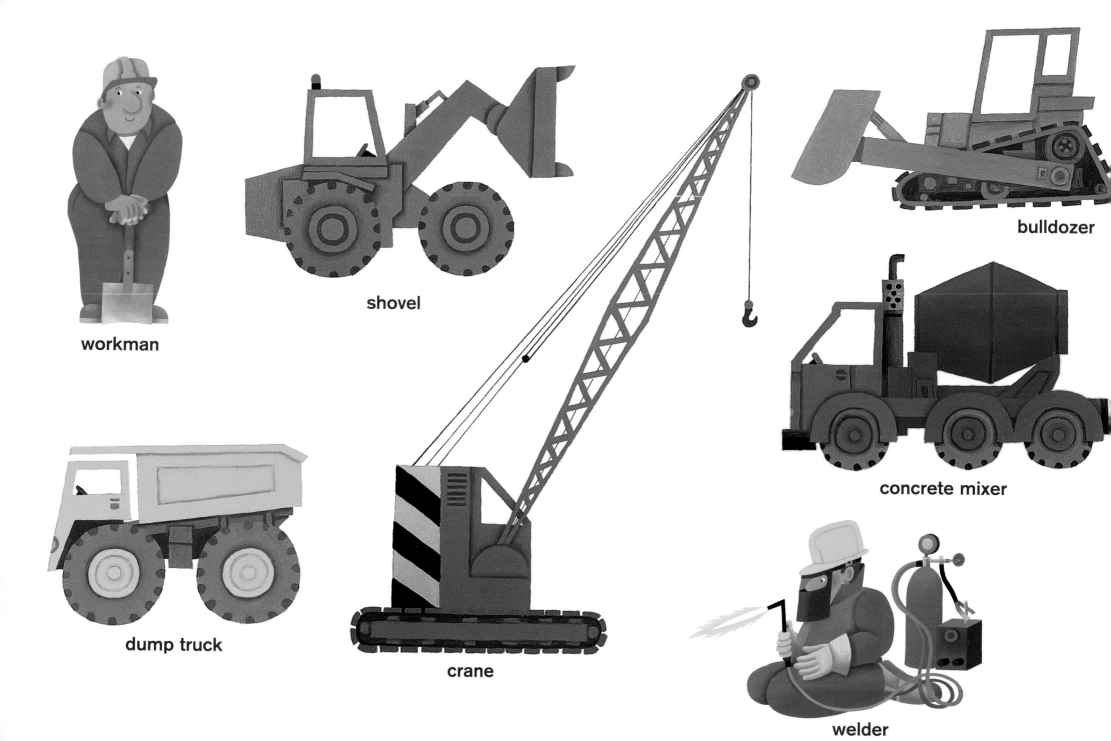

workman

shovel

bulldozer

concrete mixer

dump truck

crane

welder